THE GREAT TWIN TRICK

It's twice the fun and double the trouble for twins Jaz and Jenny when they turn a holiday for one into a holiday for two!

Mary Hooper knows more than most people what makes a good story – she's had several hundred published in teenage and women's magazines. In addition, she's the highly regarded author of over fifty titles for young people, including *Spook Spotting*; *Spooks Ahoy!*; *Best Friends, Worst Luck*; *The Boyfriend Trap*; *Mad About the Boy* and *The Peculiar Power of Tabitha Brown*.

Mary Hooper has two grown-up children, Rowan and Gemma, and lives just outside London in a small Victorian cottage.

Books by the same author

Spook Spotting

Spooks Ahoy!

For older readers

Best Friends, Worst Luck

The Boyfriend Trap

Mad About the Boy

The Peculiar Power of Tabitha Brown

THE GREAT TWIN TRICK

MARY HOOPER

Illustrations by

SUSAN HELLARD

WALKER BOOKS

AND SUBSIDIARIES

LONDON • BOSTON • SYDNEY

First published 1999 by Walker Books Ltd
87 Vauxhall Walk, London SE11 5HJ

This edition published 2000

2 4 6 8 10 9 7 5 3 1

This book has been typeset in Plantin.

Printed and bound in Great Britain by
The Guernsey Press Co. Ltd

British Library Cataloguing in Publication Data
A catalogue record for this book
is available from the British Library.

ISBN 0-7445-7737-3

Contents

Chapter 1

Jasmine and I stared out of the living-room window, faces pressed against the glass, each desperate to be the first to see the postman.

Anyone standing on the pavement would have seen two identical faces: brown eyes and freckles, short mousey hair and pigs' noses. (We don't usually have pigs' noses; this was because they were squashed to the glass.) The outside of us is identical, the inside is different. Inside, starting with me being a vegetarian and her eating every animal she can lay her hands on, we're not alike at all.

Jaz, bored with looking for the postman, turned to frown at me. "Let's get one thing straight," she said. "My poem was much better than yours."

"No it wasn't," I said. "Mine was insightful. Mum said so."

"Mine was stylish. Dad said so." Jaz put on her poetry-reading voice and declared,

"I am me.
And that's for sure.
Just don't ask me any more."

"That's not a poem," I said, still staring down the road anxiously.

At the end of summer term at school, we'd gone in for a competition to write a poem. There were four prizes of a long weekend at Paradise Park, the holiday centre which had just opened near us, and both of us had been put on a shortlist of finalists. That morning we were going to find out who'd won.

"Yours was stupid," Jaz said. "All about being a twin. *Bor–ing!*"

"Don't be so horrible," I said. "Mum said you're not to be horrible to me. She said..."

Jaz closed her eyes, put her hands over her ears and made a loud humming noise. *"Hummmmmm..."* She did this whenever I said something she didn't want to hear.

"...if you're horrible once more this week she's going to – oh, there's the postman!"

Jaz, still humming at full throttle, didn't hear, so I went to the front door and sat under the letter-box, ready. I thought about my poem:

I've got a shadow,
Someone like me,
A double, a match,
I can never be free.
She always wants to get her way,
With her I just can't win.
She drives me mad, that's what you get
When you're half a twin.

Surely, I thought, a poem like mine, an *insightful* poem, would beat a poem like Jaz's, which only had three lines.

Four letters came through the door – just as Jaz leapt into the hall.

"You didn't tell me!" she said, falling on the letters.

"Let *me!*" I said, trying to pull them out from under her. "I was here first."

"But I *got to them* first!"

"OK," I said. "Let's just look at them. We'll lay them out on the carpet..."

This we did. There were two letters for Mum – and one each for us. They were both the same: long white envelopes, typed, one to Miss Jasmine May, and one to Miss Jenny May. In the top left-hand corner they said *Holiday in Paradise!*

"Perhaps we've both won!" said Jaz.

"Or both lost."

"You open yours first."

"No, you open yours."

Jaz snatched up her envelope, ripped it open and pulled out the letter. She looked at it, gave a scream, then crumpled it into a ball. "I hate them!" she said. "I didn't want to go on the stupid holiday anyway."

I bit my lip. My turn. I opened my letter carefully and read out:

> *"Dear Jenny,*
> *Congratulations!..."*

As I said this, Jaz let out another scream.

> *"We are pleased to inform you that you are one of the winners of our poetry competition.*

As you know, the prize is a long weekend at Paradise Park, the brand-new and exciting adventure park. Full details and joining instructions are enclosed and we look forward to meeting you.

Very well done indeed!..."

I put the letter down. "Oh," I said disbelievingly. "I've won."

"You can't have," Jaz said. "There must be a mistake."

"I don't usually win things," I went on wonderingly, for it was Jaz who always did things, went in for things and won things.

"Exactly," Jaz said. She snatched the letter and scanned it carefully for signs of forgery, while I picked up the leaflet that had been sent with it.

"Listen to *this*," I said. "Log cabins set in the forest, barbecue pits, camp-fires, swimming dome, bike rides, picnics, log flumes, monorail rides."

"Sounds horrible. You'll hate it!" Jaz said.

"No I won't."

"You'll hate it without me!" she burst out.

I was just about to shout back that of course I wouldn't, it would be fantastic, *brilliant* without her there – but then I realized.

Jaz was right.

We'd never done anything like that without each other, and certainly never been on holiday apart.

"It *might* be a bit funny at first," I said, "but I'll get used to it."

"I don't think they ought to invite one twin without the other," Jaz said bitterly. "It's not fair. I think you ought to turn down the prize as a protest."

"Well! How selfish can you get!"

Jaz suddenly clutched me. "I've got an idea!"

"What?"

"It's a *fantastic* idea. Let's both go!"

I stared at her. "Don't be daft. How can we?"

"Easy," Jaz said, her eyes beginning to gleam. "We won't tell Mum and Dad that just *you've* won, so they'll take both of us there. And when we get there, I'll sneak in and then we'll just take it in turns to do things. You go swimming while I stay in; I go skating while you stay in. Easy! No one will find out!"

I gaped at her. "We can't!"

"Course we can. It'll be a laugh. Look, it's either that, or I'll be in a bad mood from now until ..." she looked at the letter, "20th August. And you don't want that, do you?"

"But we can't," I began. "What if..."

There was a noise from the back door and then Dad shouted, "Anyone home?"

"We're here!" Jaz said, jumping up.

"Have you heard? Was there anything in the post?" he called.

Jaz shook my shoulder urgently. "Are you up for it?" she hissed.

I hesitated.

"Oh, go on, Jen!" she begged, and I was so

unused to this strange happening – my sister asking me nicely, actually *pleading* for something, that I found myself nodding.

"Yes! We've both won the competition, Dad!" Jaz yelled. "We're both going to Paradise Park!"

"Ohmygod," I muttered weakly, and I squealed a frightened-mousey squeal to myself.

Chapter 2

"Nearly there," Dad said. He glanced over to me and Jaz on the back seat. (Over the years, we'd fought so much about sitting in the front that we always *both* had to go in the back.) "Now, are you sure you've got everything?"

"Sure!" we said together.

"It doesn't seem very much," he said. "Haven't you got a bag of your own, Jaz?"

Jaz shook her head. "I've put my stuff in with Jenny's."

"Why?" Dad asked.

"Because ... um ... the zip on my bag was broken," Jaz said, at the same time as I said, "Because we were told to travel light."

Dad, luckily, was busy negotiating a roundabout and didn't really hear either of us.

Actually, we'd packed a lot. And we'd brought exactly the same things to wear, of course.

Mum had been rather suspicious. "I don't know why you suddenly want to have everything the same," she'd said. "You've spent the best part of your lives trying to get out of that."

"We just want to," Jaz had said, linking her arm through mine in a display of girliness. "We want to be *real* twins."

"Hmmm..." was all Mum had said, and we were glad that she'd had to work the day we were being driven to Paradise Park. We didn't reckon we'd have been able to pull the wool over *her* eyes.

On the way there I was so nervous, it felt like ten visits to the dentist in one. To Jaz, though, it was all a laugh.

"I don't know why you're getting so jumpy about it," she whispered to me. "So what if they do find out?"

"If they find out I'll probably be carted off to prison!" I said. "It's ... it's *deception*. It's all right for you; you're not the prize-winner."

"There'll be millions of people there. They're not going to notice one extra!" she scoffed.

"No, and if they do I'll only be arrested, have my name in all the papers and be a laughing stock," I said, "so that's all right, isn't it? That doesn't..."

Her fingers went into her ears.

"Hummmmmm."

Paradise Park wasn't too long a drive – about an hour away. When we turned off the main road we drove through some woods, under an arch saying WELCOME TO PARADISE! and then up a gravelled driveway towards a semicircle of buildings. Behind these, more woods stretched into the distance, out of which rose a vast glass dome which looked like something out of a space movie. A shiny monorail snaked over the top of everything.

"It looks as if you've got a welcoming committee," Dad said, nodding ahead. "Those must be the other prize-winners."

As he spoke, Jaz dropped like a stone on to the floor of the car. We'd arranged between us that I, as the real winner of the competition, would be first to meet the officials and the other contestants. What would happen next was anyone's guess.

"Jaz? What are you doing on the floor?" said Dad, parking the car.

"Looking for something," Jaz said in a muffled voice.

"Well, find it later," Dad said. "You've got to come and meet everyone now."

"Join you in a tick," Jaz said, squashing herself even flatter on to the floor. "Go!" she hissed at me.

Feeling slightly sick, I got out of the car. Dad opened the boot and handed me the squashy nylon bag containing our clothes.

A plump woman in a green track suit waved to us. Standing behind her were two girls and a boy, and I began to walk towards them before she could walk to us.

"You must be Jenny!" the woman said heartily. She had red hair in tight curls, and a red face to match.

"That's clever," Dad said. "Sometimes

even I have trouble telling them apart!"

I froze. It had started already.

"Ah, yes," the woman said doubtfully.

"Beginner's luck, eh?" Dad said.

The woman backed slightly away from him, smiling nervously. "Er … yes," she said. "Well, I'm Polly. I'm one of the managerial staff here and I'm going to be looking after the children for the weekend." She beamed at me. "We're all going to have a jolly super time, I can tell you."

I said hello to her, and Dad shook hands. "And are these the other lucky prize-winners?" Dad asked. He glanced back at the car, obviously wondering what Jaz was doing.

"Yes, here are the other three," Polly said. "Bill, Ann and Fiona."

"Hello," Fiona said to me brightly. "You can call me Fluff." She was wearing a short black miniskirt and had curly hair which was ribbon-tied into bunches on each side of her head.

Bill, sturdy and scruffy, scowled deeply and

didn't look at me. "Aren't there any other boys?" he muttered.

Ann was neat; there was no other word to describe her. She had neatly pressed jeans, neat short hair and an earnest expression. "Pleased to meet you," she said.

For just one moment, I was glad that Jaz was around. Bill, Fluff and Ann didn't exactly look like a bundle of fun.

"Well, I'd better go and get Jaz out of the car," Dad said. "I can't think what she's doing."

I suddenly felt sick again. Polly glanced over to our car. "Actually, we don't allow dogs inside," she said.

Dad laughed. "She's been called some things but never that!"

"Ha ha," I chortled, frantically wondering how I was going to get out of this. "I don't suppose they allow cats either, do they? Or rats or gerbils or hamsters or chinchillas or minks or swans or bandicoots or ... or ... albatrosses!"

There was a moment's silence while everyone looked at me. Then Polly said quickly, "I think we'd better go and find our chalet now."

"I hope there's boys inside there," Bill said darkly. "I'm not stopping if there's not boys."

Dad said, "I'll just go and..."

"No, I'll go!" I interrupted hurriedly. "I'll go now and ... er ... be back soon."

"What?" Dad asked in confusion, and as I scurried to the car, I heard him ask Polly if she wanted him to go in with us.

"No," she said, "they'll all be perfectly all right with me."

Back at the car, I told Jaz that she was to get out *now*. As I turned back to join the others she, under cover of the car and bent double, ran across the drive into one of the shops in the reception area. In spite of feeling very squealy-mousey indeed, I also felt a bit smug: this was the first time within living memory that Jaz had done something to my command.

"Paradise Parks have the highest safety standards," Polly was saying to Dad as I got back to the little group.

"Yes – good," Dad said vaguely. "So I'll just pick the girls up on Monday. Six o'clock at the main gates, OK?"

"The *girls?*" Polly laughed. "I'm afraid you won't be able to take Ann and Fiona. They're being collected by their own parents!"

As Dad looked at her blankly, inspiration hit me and I pulled at his jacket. "Dad!" I hissed. "Can we have a word?"

He stepped aside from the others. "What is it? Where's Jaz? And what's wrong with this Polly woman – is she mad?"

"Jaz had an urgent call for the loo!" I whispered.

"What?"

"Dad! It's embarrassing. Jaz desperately wanted the loo so she's gone off and says goodbye to you."

He rolled his eyes but bent to kiss me anyway. "OK, then," he said. "Take care." He turned back to Polly and the others. "I'm off now," he said. "I hope you all have a good time."

As he made his way to the car, I saw Jaz inside the shop, half hidden behind an advertisement placard and taking an interest in a souvenir tea towel.

Polly led me, Bill, Ann and Fluff through the entrance, explaining to the man on the gate that we were the competition winners. There were lots of other people coming and going, and as she led the way through the trees into the camp, I hung back for a moment, pretending to be fiddling with the zip on my bag. The one thing that Jaz and I had planned was that I should somehow make myself memorable to whoever let us in: the man on the gate.

"It's a *lovely* place, isn't it?" I said to him now.

He nodded.

"And what a lovely job you've got," I went on. "With a lovely uniform."

The man raised his eyebrows but didn't say anything.

"Yes, it's all lovely, lovely, lovely," I said, smiling until my face ached and unable to think of anything else to say.

"Come along, Jenny!" Polly called, and Ann turned to stare at me sternly.

I went along. A little further on, the road branched into three. One way led towards the glass-topped dome – which I could now see contained water flumes and towers – another towards some funfair type things; the third had a sign which said *Sleepy Valley Holiday Village*.

This was the road we took. Would Jaz get in, I wondered, or would she have to remain stuck behind that tea towel for the rest of the weekend?

Chapter 3

"Now, we've got a family chalet," Polly said, standing in the hall of one of Paradise Park's Luxury Home-from-Home Holiday Ranchettes, "so everyone's got their own super room."

I heaved a sigh of relief. I'd been worried in case I'd have to share with someone else, which would have meant that Jaz and I would have to sleep in shifts of four hours each.

"The bedrooms are identical, so I'll just number you off." Polly tapped our heads in turn, "One, two, three, four."

I got Room 2, next to the shower and opposite the living-room. It was painted bright green and contained a narrow bed, a small wardrobe and a chest of drawers. It also had a window. I opened this and stuck my head out, looking for Jaz. Where had she gone? Had she managed to get in yet?

I opened the wardrobe and threw in the squashy bag, then went into the living-room, where Polly and the others were. This room had a big table and chairs, a TV, three sofas and some easy chairs. On two sides were windows looking out on to other Luxury Home-from-Home Holiday Ranchettes.

"I'll leave you four to get to know each other while I go up to the office and let them know you've arrived safely," Polly said. "We've got to have our official photographer around at some time to take pictures of you lucky prize-winners for the local papers!"

I smiled uneasily, thinking ahead, thinking of a photo appearing in our local paper, and of Mum asking why Jaz wasn't in it; thinking of me saying that she'd been busy at the time and Mum saying how ridiculous and why couldn't Paradise Park have made sure she'd been there and how she was going to contact them, and then *them* saying what did she mean why wasn't Jaz in it, who was Jaz? And so on until everything was discovered.

As Polly went out, the four of us stared at each other.

"They told me there would be another boy," Bill said, and he turned his back, brought out a pocket Game Boy and started pushing buttons which made noises.

"Do you like kittens?" Fluff asked me and Ann.

We nodded.

"Do you?" she asked Bill.

"They're all right," Bill said gruffly.

"I *love* kittens," Fluff said. "My poem was about kittens."

"Mine was about Life," Ann said earnestly. "It had sixteen verses, each of seven lines, about the growth stages of Woman. My English teacher at school said it was very accomplished."

I was doing my best to look interested when suddenly I froze, seeing Jaz's head slowly appear above the window-sill behind Ann and Fluff. Her face had a big smile on it. "Found you!" she mouthed.

Although inside I was squealy-mousey, thinking *ohmygodwhatamIgoingtodo!*, outside I had to struggle to keep the same expression on my face. As Ann was still speaking, this was a bored look.

"Some of it rhymes, and some is blank verse, which makes a harsh contrast to the more lyrical parts," she went on.

"Let me in!" Jaz mouthed, pointing towards the front door.

"This in turn reflects some of the qualities of Life," Ann droned, while Fluff looked at her, fluffy and puzzled.

"Wait," I mouthed at Jaz, trying to make the word as much as possible into a yawn.

Ann finished speaking at last.

"Puppies are nice, too. But not as nice as kittens," Fluff put in quickly. "Do you like puppies, Bill?"

"They're all right," Bill said gruffly, between *beeps*.

"Do you like them, Jenny?"

Jaz began to hop up and down outside the window impatiently.

"Hurry!" she said, and luckily there was piped music inside the chalet, so no one could hear. "Hurry!"

"I can't!" I blurted out.

Fluff blinked, and both she and Ann looked at me curiously.

"You can't?" Fluff asked. "How d'you mean, you can't like puppies?"

"Well, I ... er ... would like to like them, but I can't because I'm allergic to them," I said. "The fur, you know."

"Oh, that's a shame," Fluff said. "Are you allergic to kittens, too?"

"No, not kittens," I said.

Ann looked serious. "I wouldn't have thought that whether or not you were allergic to something prevented you from liking it."

"No. I suppose not," I said meekly.

"Would you like to hear my poem about kittens?" Fluff asked, and without waiting for a reply, began,

"Kittens are cute,
Kittens like fruit,
Kittens are dear little things..."

Ann stood politely listening, while Bill hunched further over his game. Outside, to my absolute horror, I saw Polly suddenly appear round the nearest ranchette and head straight for this one – *and Jaz*...

"Hello, Jenny!" I saw Polly say. "Having a look around?"

Jaz said something I couldn't hear.

Polly put her hand on her shoulder. "Coming back inside to hear all the super things we've got planned?"

I froze for a split second, and then immediately sprang into action. "I'm going to unpack!" I announced to the others, not caring that Fluff was mid-kitten. I leapt out of the living-room and into the hall, disappearing into Room 2 just a moment before Polly and Jaz came into the hall together.

I heard Polly say something about them having lots of fun in store for us, and then they went into the living-room. I pressed my ear to the bedroom door, squirming, waiting for Jaz to drop us both in it.

"That was quick!" I heard Ann say. "You can't have hung your clothes up already. Not on hangers."

"You missed the end of my kitten poem," Fluff said. "Shall I begin it again?"

I didn't hear what the others replied to this, but Polly said, "Now, as far as tomorrow's activities go..."

"Oh, can you wait a minute?" Jaz interrupted her. "I've just remembered that I didn't hang my clothes up properly."

"I knew you couldn't have," said Ann. "Not that quickly."

"Perhaps you can do them later," Polly suggested.

"No, I *must* do them now," Jaz said. Then she added, "I've forgotten which was my room."

"How *can* you have?" Ann asked, "you've only just come from there."

"It's Room 2," Polly said. "Do be quick."

"Kittens are cute,
Kittens like fruit..."

Fluff began again.

"Won't be long!" I heard Jaz say.

She came into the bedroom, punching the air. "Yeah!"

"Ssshhh!" I said nervously.

"Hey, it looks really good out there, doesn't it?" said Jaz. "I can't wait to go on things."

"Never mind going on things," I said, "just remember that if you hear anyone coming, you're to hide. Get in the wardrobe."

"Wouldn't be able to breathe in there."

"Under the bed, then. Look, the woman's name is Polly."

"Yeah, super Polly – met her."

"And there's Fluff, Ann and Bill. Ann is the neat and tidy one, Fluff is…"

"Yes, yes," Jaz said, "I think I can work out which one's Fluff and which one's Bill. Now, what are we going to do about eating? I'm starving."

"When we go out to eat, I'll bring you something back," I said. "You'll just have to wait here for me, very quietly."

As I spoke, I sighed. Waiting very quietly wasn't Jaz's thing, and there were three whole nights and three whole days to get through yet…

Chapter 4

"Now, we've got several groups from schools here this weekend," Polly said.

"Bet they're not boys' schools," Bill said dourly.

We'd all been given fifteen minutes' unpacking time and were back in the living-room. Jaz was in my bedroom, having promised not to move, breathe or make any sound whatsoever on penalty of instant death.

"They're from *mixed* schools," said Polly. "And we've got lots of family groups here as well. With boys," she added. She beamed at us. "The emphasis at Paradise Parks is on having fun! There are lots of things to do and lots of prizes to be won!"

I didn't say anything, just thought to myself that it was going to be hard enough getting through the weekend without bothering about winning prizes.

"What sort of prizes?" Bill asked. "Are they *boys'* prizes?"

"They're suitable for everyone," Polly said. "There are computer games and footballs and CDs and tennis rackets and trendy sportswear and all sorts of super things!"

"Kittens?" Fluff asked.

"Everything except kittens," Polly said. She waved a list of events in the air. "Your weekend is going to be packed with fun, ending with the Monday Marathon right round the grounds on your last day. And for you competition winners, everything is free."

"Do we get free food? Are we going to eat now?" Bill asked.

"Quite soon," Polly said. "Now, tomorrow morning we'll be going along to Paradise Pools. There are flumes and river rides and a diving pool and a steam room and lots of watery activities."

"I'm *starving!*" Bill said.

"And then in the afternoon..."

"Agghhh," Bill said, clutching his stomach and rolling on to the floor.

Polly looked startled. "Are you all right, Bill?"

He looked up. "No, I'm starving."

"OK," Polly said. "We'll go over to Paradise Diner now and you can order whatever you like!"

Before we set off, I went to get my track suit top, which I knew was big and billowy enough to hide a couple of extra packets of chips. OK, they'd be cold by the time we got back, but Jaz would just have to put up with that. Cold chips was a small price to pay for a free holiday.

I went into the bedroom. "It's only me. We're going out for food," I whispered.

There was no reply. I looked all round, in the wardrobe and under the bed, but there was no sign of her.

On the chest of drawers, though, was a note. It said: *Bored with being stuck in here. Gone to eat. J.*

I nearly screamed. She'd *promised* to stay where she was!

Fluff came in while I was reading the note. "Are you ready?" she said. "What are you wearing? I didn't know whether to change or not, so I've just put on my pink sweatshirt. It's got kittens on the front," she added unnecessarily.

Before I could scrumple up the note, she'd looked at it over my shoulder. "Ooh, are you bored with being here? Is it because of Ann and her poem? Doesn't it sound awful? Why have you written that note to yourself?"

"To … er … just to remind myself where I'm going," I said.

She blinked. "But you haven't gone anywhere yet. We're going *now*."

"Well, it's notes for my diary," I said.

"But why have you written them in advance?"

"Just because…" I floundered. I stared at her desperately. "What a lovely sweatshirt!" I blurted. "Are they Persian kittens or Siamese kittens on it? Which d'you think are nicer?"

"Oh, Persians!" she said immediately. "Because they're fluffier. And they've got such dear little squashed-up faces."

"And Siamese kittens do that awful

yowling, don't they?" I said. "And they grow up into Siamese cats, and I'm not too keen on them because they're cross-eyed and…" As I waffled madly, I steered her through my bedroom door and into the hall, where Polly and the others were waiting.

It took us about ten minutes to walk to Paradise Diner. On the way, Polly pointed out some of the attractions: the roller-skating rink, the log flume, the rock-climbing mountain and the cycling circuit. It all looked good, actually – quite exciting – but I couldn't take in what she was saying because I was too scared that at any minute we were going to bump into Jaz.

Paradise Diner was bright and shiny and red and white. It had a long counter area on one side where you queued up and selected your food, and masses of tables and chairs.

As I looked round for Jaz, my heart was thumping heavily. When I didn't see her, though, I began to relax a bit. It might be all right, because Polly had told us that there were three other cafés and restaurants. With a bit of luck, she'd be in one of those, or maybe she'd just got a sandwich from the takeaway bar and gone back.

We queued for our food, discussing what we were going to eat, while Polly explained to the women behind the counter that we were the super competition winners and could have anything we wanted.

"I hope there's a vegetarian selection," Ann said, sniffing the air. "And that it's not *all* junk food."

I licked my lips. "I'm a veggie, too," I said, "but apart from that, I don't care what I have as long as there's lots of it."

We shuffled along to the food displays. Bill took something from nearly every serving tray, Fluff had fish fingers and Ann had a small, neat omelette cooked specially for her. I was last in line, and asked the woman serving for two veggie-burgers and double chips.

"I'm really hungry," I explained to her.

She raised her eyebrows. "You must be," she said. "This is the second time you've been in!"

Inside, I was making the squealy-mouse noise. Outside, I was saying, "I … well … no, it isn't."

"Oh yes it is!"

"You must be mistaken," I blabbered, and I tried to squish my face up at one side so that I looked entirely different.

"No, I'm not," she said. "You're one of the poetry competition winners, aren't you? You told me all about it – don't you remember?"

"Um … I…"

"And you had a large pizza with extra chilli meat topping!"

"You said you were a vegetarian!" Ann said accusingly.

"How did you get over here without us?" Fluff asked.

I swallowed. "I … er … don't say anything to Polly, will you?" I said in a low voice. "I was so hungry I popped out and ran over here while we were supposed to be unpacking."

"It's no skin off my nose," said the woman behind the counter, shovelling chips. "I like to see a youngster with a good appetite."

As I reached for my veggie-burgers, Ann was still looking at me reproachfully.

"I *am* a vegetarian," I said to her. "It's just that occasionally I eat meat."

"Then you're not a vegetarian."

"I am mostly," I said. I carried my tray over to our table, where Bill was already tucking into a food mountain. I began to move a burger towards the edge of the table ready to hide under my track suit – and then I remembered that Jaz had already eaten, and moved it back again. I was going to eat her portion as well as mine, and serve her right.

"But your principles shouldn't allow you to eat meat! Not ever!" Ann went on, all of a quiver. "I don't know how you can possibly..."

She looked as if she could go on all evening so I turned in desperation to Fluff. "I'd *love* to hear your kitten poem again."

Halfway through a fish finger she began,

"Kittens are cute,
Kittens like fruit..."

Chapter 5

"I haven't slept a wink," Jaz said the next morning.

"Sshh!"

"I haven't slept a wink," she whispered. "You've taken up all the bed. All night. And all the duvet."

"It's my bed," I said. "I'm the prize-winner so it's my bed and my duvet."

"I'm just going to have to stay here and sleep all day and try to catch up, then."

"That's good," I said, "because if you're sleeping you won't be rushing all over the place pretending to be me and eating meat."

"I had to eat, didn't I?" she grumbled. "I would have starved to death if I'd waited any longer."

"Sshh!"

From the next-door bathroom came the sound of water gurgling. "I'm going in the shower," I said, "so just in case anyone comes in, I want you to lie here without moving, with the duvet pulled right up and the pillow over you."

"I might suffocate," she said as I covered her up.

"Well, if you do," I whispered, "do it quietly."

I had a quick shower, getting out of the bathroom and back in the bedroom in a couple of minutes. Jaz was out of bed, still in her pyjamas and looking out of the window.

"I told you to stay in bed!" I hissed. I dried myself and pulled on leggings and a T-shirt.

"No one's going to come in!" she said.

I went to the wardrobe to get a jumper. "Remember to put on everything the same as me, right? And how can you be sure that no one's going to come in. They might."

"As if someone's going to..." she began scornfully – just as the bedroom door opened. She was nearest to it; I was by the wardrobe. With one hand she pushed me in and shut the door on me.

"Jenny," I heard Fluff say, "would you like to look at my kitten catalogue?" She giggled.

"I call it that because it's photographs of kittens that I've collected from magazines. My CATalogue, see!"

"Ha ha," Jaz laughed falsely.

"I'm letting *you* look at it first."

"It sounds really interesting," Jaz lied, "but I'm just about to go in the shower. I'll look at it another time."

"But you've just had a shower," Fluff said. "I saw you coming out of the bathroom."

In the darkness of the wardrobe, I felt myself go clammy all over.

"That wasn't me," Jaz said. "It must have been someone else."

"But the someone came in here!" There was a pause. "And look, your towel's all wet!"

"Er..." Jaz began.

"Oh, I know," Fluff said helpfully, "you forgot what your room number was yesterday, didn't you? So perhaps you've forgotten that you've already had a shower."

"That's it!" Jaz said. "That's exactly what's happened."

Inside the wardrobe, I quietly sighed with relief.

"What a lovely sweatshirt," I heard Jaz say. "It's got little fluffy kittens on it. Is that real fur?"

"It's the same one I had on last night," Fluff said. "Because you asked me about Persian kittens and Siamese kittens, don't you remember?"

"Ah, yes. Course I did."

"You *do* keep forgetting things, don't you? I think you're a bit of a catastrophe," Fluff giggled. "CATastrophe, get it?"

Jaz gave another false laugh.

"So do you want to look at my kitten pictures now?"

"I would, but I'm just going to have a shower," Jaz said. "I know I've already had one, but because I've forgotten it, it doesn't count."

"Oh," Fluff said.

"I'll see you later!"

There was the sound of someone leaving –

two people leaving – and then the bathroom door opened and closed as Jaz went in. Cautiously, I let myself out of the wardrobe – just as Polly banged on the bedroom door and opened it.

"Morning, Jenny. Breakfast in two minutes!" she said. "Coming through?"

Starting back in shock, I made the terrified squealy-mouse noise. At this rate I was going to be dead of fright before the weekend was over.

Polly looked at me closely. "All right this morning, are we?" she asked, shaking her red curls at me.

"Yes," I gulped. "Be with you in a minute."

Jaz was still in the bathroom, of course, so I quickly wrote her a note saying I'd gone to breakfast and if she moved from the bedroom I would personally kill her. I then took a deep breath and went through to the living-room.

Closing the door firmly behind me, I went to sit at the table, which was piled with the sort of breakfasty foods you get on holiday:

fruit, loads of different cereals, rolls, crumpets.

Fluff's jaw dropped on seeing me. "That was fast!" she said. "How did you manage to shower as quickly as that?"

"Well," I said, "I remembered about the first shower, so in the end I didn't need the other one."

Fluff looked at me fluffily. As well she might.

Polly came in from the kitchen with a big china dish. "Now, I've cooked a lovely pile of scrambled eggs, bacon and mushrooms," she said. "This will give you lots of energy for all the super things we're going to do today."

Ann looked at me severely. "I suppose you're a bacon-eating vegetarian, are you?"

"Not this morning," I said.

While we were eating and talking about such topics as what kittens like for breakfast, how much sleep kittens have and why tortoiseshell kittens are always girls, there was a sudden loud noise from the bathroom. A noise of someone bursting out singing and then stopping abruptly when realizing that they shouldn't.

"What was *that*?" Polly asked, buttering a pile of toast.

"I think it was … er … my musical alarm clock," I said. "It keeps going funny." While they were all looking towards the door, I whipped two pieces of toast off the pile and hid them under my jumper. "I'll just go and sort it out!"

I stretched out in the Jacuzzi and tried to breathe deeply and relax. It was difficult, because I was waiting for someone to come up at any moment and say how *could* I be there, because they'd just that minute seen me in the swimming-pool or roller-skating or eating a meaty pie with extra meat or something.

It honestly wasn't fair! While I was wearing myself out to a frazzle covering up for Jaz, making plans, smoothing things over, stuffing toast up my jumper and inventing excuses, *she* was just swanning about the place enjoying herself.

Earlier that morning, we'd gone roller-skating. Bill had been really good at it and had won a speed prize, and Fluff wasn't bad, but Ann and I had been useless. This had led to Bill going on and on about how all girls were crabby at sport, and how all boys, especially him, were excellent. Ann had had a real go at him, and Fluff had just giggled, but I'd been too busy looking over my shoulder and everyone else's shoulder to bother to say anything. A little get-back-at-him idea began forming at the back of my head, though. *There were two of me, and he didn't know it.*

Just then, a figure in a pink Lurex bikini slipped into the Jacuzzi beside me.

"Will oo come in the steam room with me?" Fluff asked in a ickle baby voice. "Only it's all quiet and foggy in there and I'm a bit scared to go on my own."

I stole a quick look round. The Jacuzzi,

together with the steam room, sauna and beauty salons, was in a small unit off the crowded main swimming-pool area. Various people padded about, but the coast looked clear. I hauled myself out of the water and went with her.

"Oooh, isn't it spooky in here!" she said as we went into the steam room.

It was. It was also so hot and wet and misty that it made you gasp when you breathed in. It was quite a small room, made of marble, and had stone benches with great puffs of steam coming from underneath them. You couldn't see to the other side, but had to grope your way to a bench to sit down.

"I hope this won't make my hair go all funny," Fluff said. Then she added, "I wonder what this spooky mist is supposed to *do*."

From out of the mist and from the other side of the room came a voice. "It's supposed to be good for your skin," Jaz said.

I froze.

Fluff jumped. "I didn't think there was anyone else here!"

"Only me!" Jaz said cheerily.

Fluff nudged me. "Whoever that is, sounds just like you."

"I don't think so," I said. I was going to *kill* Jaz when I got her on her own.

"I don't think so!" said the echo, sounding *exactly* like me.

"Oooh–er," Fluff said, trying to peer through the fog. "I don't like it in here. It's like there's a ghost or something."

"Yes, I am Jenny's ghost!" came the voice.

"Oooh!" went Fluff.

"But I'm not dead!" I objected.

"The ghost of Jenny's *future*," said Jaz.

"But … but…" Fluff stuttered.

"How ridiculous!" I said. "Someone's playing tricks on us – and your hair *is* going funny. Shall we try the sauna?"

Chapter 6

"That was fantastic!" I said, heaving myself, soaking wet, out of the flume boat thingy and leaning on the wall to try and get my breath back.

It was later the same day and we – Fluff, Bill, Ann and I – had been on the log flume four times now. Bill said it wasn't as high as one he'd been on in Blackpool, Ann said she didn't really *like* them but she didn't want to spoil it for the rest of us, and Fluff didn't say anything, she just screamed from the beginning of the ride to the end.

As we were staggering round to rejoin the queue yet again, Polly came up and asked us if we wanted something to eat.

Bill said he was starving to death, and the rest of us said we could manage a bag of chips, so we hung around watching everyone else while Polly went to get supplies from one of the Paradise takeaways.

I'd moved from the queue and was standing beside a small ice-cream kiosk, which happened to be closed, when I heard a *psstt*.

It was Jaz, peering out of a crack in the kiosk door.

I walked round to the side where I couldn't be seen by the others. "What d'you want?" I asked. "And what are you doing here anyway? You promised to stay out of sight *all day*."

"I want a go on that log flume," Jaz said.

"You can have a go later," I muttered out of the side of my mouth.

"You've had twelve goes!"

"I've had *four*."

"Well, it seems like twelve. I'm bored," she said. "I want to go on now. You could easily let me have the next go. No one would know."

While she was speaking she was opening the kiosk door wider and wider, moving slowly out.

"Go back in!" I said, pushing at the door.

"Don't be mean. Let me have a go." She carried on opening the door, revealing more and more of herself to the outside world.

I groaned. I *knew* she wasn't going to go back again, so I glanced round to make sure no one was watching, then squeezed in myself. We were like two people on a weatherclock: as I went in, Jaz came out – *sauntered* out, cool as anything – and went across to the others.

I watched through a knot-hole in the wood. At first I thought it was going to be OK, but then I noticed all three of them were staring at her.

What was wrong? I checked her all over, bit by bit. We were wearing identical black leggings, white T-shirts and grubby white trainers, and our hair was exactly the same style and everything. It wasn't any of *those* things.

As Fluff began circling around Jaz, looking confused, the squealy-mouse noise started in the back of my throat. What *was* it?

Ann was frowning. Bill looked fierce. What on earth were they looking at that I hadn't noticed?

And then I realized.

"How did you get dry that quickly?" Fluff asked.

"You've been back to change!" Bill jeered. "Couldn't stand your clothes being wet – you … you *girl!*" he said.

"She can't have been back to the chalet," Ann said. "She's been standing just by the kiosk all the time."

Just then, Polly came up with bags of chips which she distributed round, telling them what super ones they were. She looked at Jaz and her jaw dropped. "Jenny, how *did* you get dry so quickly? You were the wettest of all."

"Well, I raced about," Jaz said, waving her arms round her head like a windmill and doing jumping jacks. "Like this. Everything just dried off in seconds."

Polly shook her head, puzzled. "I can't understand it. You must have terribly hot blood. You must be like a convector heater."

"That's right," Jaz nodded, scoffing my chips as fast as she could while jumping on the spot. "Just like a radiator, me!"

"Are we going back in the queue?" Bill asked huffily. "Only while you've been talking about people getting wet and dry, a whole girls' school has gone in front of us."

"We're having a camp-fire tonight," I whispered to Jaz, back in the bedroom much later, after a swimming competition which Bill had won hands down. "A camp-fire, barbecue and sing-song."

"That sounds good," she said.

"Not *you*, you're not having it," I said. "*We're* having a camp-fire – the prize-winners. So *you* can go anywhere you like in Paradise Park and eat as much chilli pizza as you want. You can eat chilli pizza all night if you like, just keep away from me."

She considered this. "I'd rather stay round the camp-fire, cooking things."

"Well, you can't!" I said fiercely. I pulled on a thick jumper ready for the great out-doors. "Just stay away and out of sight, OK?"

"OK!" she said.

I looked at her suspiciously. She'd given in much too easily…

Chapter 7

It was Sunday morning and raining in Paradise. It had started raining the night before, actually, in the middle of the jolly sing-song, but I'd been quite relieved to go indoors because from somewhere behind us in the bushes I'd kept hearing another voice, very out of tune, joining in. Polly had said it was just someone being silly, and to ignore them.

I hadn't said anything, but quietly *glowered* with rage.

We were supposed to be going on a bike ride around the Park that morning, but while we waited for the rain to stop, Polly suggested that we each read out the poem that we'd won the competition with.

"Although maybe you, Fluff, would like to recite something different," she added. "I think I already know *Kittens Are Cute* off by heart."

I looked out of the window. I badly wanted to go out because in Room 2, hanging about like a caged tiger, was Jaz, and I was terrified that any minute she was going to do something to give us away.

"Polly, I hope you don't mind me asking," Ann said, "but were our poems chosen from hundreds and hundreds?"

"Well, um…" Polly said.

"Were they chosen from *millions*?" Fluff asked eagerly.

"Well, not exactly millions," Polly said. "About twelve."

"Twelve hundred?" I asked.

"No. Just twelve," said Polly.

"What!" we all said, and I, for one, was severely disappointed. There was me thinking that I was a genius.

"I don't think the competition got enough publicity," Polly went on. "We had to choose the best from the very few entries we had."

She turned to Bill and slapped him on the back. "Shall we have yours now, Bill? I expect you've written something about football and wild animals, eh? Is yours a good laddish poem?"

"Dunno what you'd call it," Bill said. "My mum wrote it."

We all stared at him.

"Oooh!" Fluff said.

Polly coughed. "I'll pretend I didn't hear that, Bill," she said. "I'm sure you just mean that your mum helped you with a couple of words."

"No, I don't," Bill said.

"Yes, you do," Polly said firmly, going rather red in the face, "because if she had written it, I'd have to send you home at once and you wouldn't get to run in the Monday Marathon."

"OK," said Bill.

Polly turned to me and Ann. "Now, who's going to be next?"

"The twelve ages of woman..."

Ann began solemnly, and Polly said, "Oh, look outside – I do think it's clearing up, so there might not be quite time enough for all that … er … super epic, Ann. Shall we have Jenny's instead?"

"Mine's only short," I said. "It's called 'My Other Half'.

"I've got a shadow,
Someone like me,
A double, a match,
I can never be free.
She always wants to get her way,
With her I just can't win.
She drives me mad, that's what you get
When you're half a…"

Just as I was about to say it, I suddenly realized and came to a shuddering halt. I couldn't say *twin*! If I did, then they might put two and two together and realize why a lot of strange things had happened. *"Half a… Half a…"* I floundered.

Everyone was staring at me.

"Oh dear," I said, "I seem to have forgotten the last word."

"You can't have!" said Polly.

"I don't really understand what it means," Fluff said happily.

"There are only so many words it could be," Ann said. "Half a *pin* or half a *bin* or..."

Thankfully, brilliantly, just then the sun came out. "Oh look – it really has cleared up!" I said. "Shall we go and get the bikes?"

Red-faced and flustered, I went into the bedroom to get changed. Jaz was stretched out on the floor under cover of the bed, reading a magazine and eating a bar of chocolate.

"I'm never going to let you talk me into anything like this ever again!" I said. "All *you* have to do is lounge about the place, stuff yourself with food and join in singing from bushes. It's *me* who has all the covering up to worry about, *me* who has to keep making excuses and *me* who has to pretend to keep forgetting things."

"This is true," she said, turning a page of her mag.

"I reckon you owe me a great big favour for letting you come here! When we get home I think you ought to do all our jobs for a month."

"Two days," she said. *"Hummmmmm."*

"Jenny!" Polly called from the hall. "Are you talking to yourself in there? The rest of us are changed and ready."

"Just coming!" I called back.

We rode our bikes right round the outside of the Park, twice, and when we stopped for a breather Polly told us that we'd be following the same course for the marathon tomorrow, which was (thank goodness) our last day.

"Our Monday Marathon is really super fun," she said. "Nearly all the under-sixteens go in for it and we have a marked route and drinks along the way, just like a real marathon."

"And prizes?" Bill asked.

"Yes, lots of prizes," Polly said.

"I'm excellent at running," Bill said. "I ran

for our school in the County Finals."

I was about to say something like *so what?* or *big deal*, but then it suddenly came to me: what Jaz and I could do to get one over on Bill...

I smiled at him wistfully. "It must be really nice to be a boy and good at things."

"Yeah, well," he said, "girls are no good at running, are they? They're not built for it."

"They've got better things to do," said Ann.

"Well, we won't argue about it, will we?" Polly said. "We'll just take our bikes back to the hire centre now, because after that super ride I expect you'd all like a rest."

"Rest!" Bill said. "I ride twenty times longer than this at home. Forty times!"

"Fantastic..." I murmured admiringly. Oh yes, Bill, I thought, I'm going to sort you out good and proper...

That night after lights-out, I outlined my plan to Jaz. She agreed with me that Bill was big-headed and insufferable and that it would be a *wonderful* lesson for him if he was beaten in the Monday Marathon. And by a girl. Or by two girls: I was going to start the marathon, and Jaz was going to finish it!

"OK," I whispered, tugging to try and get a morsel of duvet for myself, "now let's go over what we're going to do."

She tugged the duvet back. "*You're* going to line up and start with all the others."

I nodded. "We're off at two o'clock and the start is at the big entrance gates. Everyone runs right round the outside edge of the Park, in and out of the ornamental gardens and into the woods. No one can get lost because there are flags marking the way."

"When you get into the woods," Jaz continued, "you're going to sprint off and hide."

"Yes," I nodded, "and *you're* going to be hiding somewhere near the finish – which is at the flagpole on the hill – and just at the right moment..."

"I'm going to run out and win! Yeah!" She punched the air and pulled even more duvet.

"Ssshh!" I said, for I could hear Polly still moving about the ranchette. "Now, we know the record time is forty-five minutes, and Bill said he wants to match that record, so I reckon we should..."

"...break it," Jaz said.

"Right," I whispered. "If we start at two o'clock, you could run out and win at exactly two forty-one."

"Two forty-one. Synchronize watches!" Jaz said.

We did this, and then we slapped hands, which meant she had to let go of the duvet for an instant. I pulled it, she pulled back violently, and somehow I ended up on the floor with a thud.

"Are you all right in there?" Polly called.

A hand came over my mouth. "Fine, thank you, Polly!" Jaz said. "Just doing my exercises ready for the marathon."

Chapter 8

Monday, our last day, and although Paradise Park had been exciting, mostly it had been just a bit *too* exciting. I was really looking forward to getting home again.

Before that, of course, before Dad came to pick us up at six o'clock, there was the marathon.

That morning we four prize-winners had spent hours riding on the monorail and having log flume rides, while Jaz had stayed out of the way in the swimming dome. Straight after lunch she and I met in the bedroom and had a last-minute check of everything.

We went over the timings again, made sure that we were both wearing exactly the same, that our hair was identical and that neither of us had even a freckle out of place.

"So after the prize-giving at four o'clock," I said finally, "you're going to hang about a bit and lord it over Bill, then go to the main gates to wait for Dad. I'll appear back at the ranchette, say goodbye to Polly and the others and …" I breathed a sigh of relief "… then it will all be over and we can go home."

"You needn't sound so pleased about it," Jaz said. "I think it's been really fun."

"Sort of," I shuddered.

At one-thirty she put on her jogging top and pulled the hood well down over her head, so that our own mum wouldn't even know her.

She heaved herself on to the window-sill. "OK, I'm off!"

"We haven't spoken about the prize," I hissed. "If you get the choice, get roller-blades."

"Won't!"

"You said you…" I began – but she was over the sill and away.

I went to join the others and just before two o'clock, Polly took us over to the start of the marathon and enrolled us. She gave us a pep talk and left us there with the other runners, saying that she'd see us later.

"I don't know why you girls are bothering,"

Bill said, doing extravagant leg stretches as we waited. He'd been what he called "in training" all over the place that morning: doing press-ups, racing around like a greyhound and bending over trying to touch his toes with his elbows.

"I'm only going to run until I get out of breath," Ann said.

"Oh, typical!" Bill jeered.

"I'll probably carry on until the end," I said casually. "I mean, it's just a bit of fun, isn't it?"

"You won't win," Bill said to me as he lifted his knee to his chin. "You won't come anywhere near."

"Oh, I know that," I said, gazing at Bill with fake admiration. "I mean, how could I beat all these boys? How could I beat *you*?"

"Exactly," he said.

Fluff sidled up to me. "Can I run with you?" she said.

I jumped and stared at her in horror. "Well, I..."

“I want to run all the way with you. We can pace each other like they do in real races.”

“I’m er … not sure,” I said.

“Oh go on! That’s settled, then,” she said, squeezing herself next to me on the starting line.

There were about forty entrants altogether, and the race began properly with a real starting gun and everyone cheering. Bill sprinted off straight away, ahead of everyone else, and the rest of us tracked him at our own pace along the fence, following the marker flags through the gardens. By the time the first pack reached the winding track that led into the woods, Ann and some others had already packed up, and most of those who were left were quite spread out.

Not me and Fluff, though. She’d stuck to me every inch of the way, talking non-stop kitten.

I began to get out of breath and into panic. If I couldn’t shake Fluff off, then the whole plan would fall down and Jaz and I would be exposed. I thought about fainting, or pretending to twist my ankle – but if I did that she'd stay with me and call for help. What was I going to *do*...?

And then it came to me.

"By the way," I puffed, "I heard one of the other runners talking about the pets' corner here."

"Mmm?" she said. "It's all right, that pets' corner, but it's all llamas and lambs and stuff. I don't think you should have a pets' corner without..."

"That's just it," I said, crossing my fingers. "Apparently they're having a delivery of kittens today. I meant to tell you earlier but I..."

But she'd gone. Vanished into the distance.

My next problem was the spectators lining the edge of the track, but luckily, the deeper we got into the woods, the fewer of these there were. Eventually, the only person in sight was a woman waving drinks about. I ran past her, pushed myself into a bush and just sat there until the coast was completely clear. Once I was sure that it was, I took my hooded top from round my waist and put it on, pulling the hood right over my head as Jaz had done. Then I took off my shorts and put on a pair of leggings so that Jaz and I would look as different as possible.

I checked my watch. It was two-thirty and time to make my way to the finish of the marathon. But I was going the short way!

Keeping my head well down, I nipped across the grounds towards the flagpole on the hill. A striped tent had been erected here, and a crowd had already gathered. There were banners saying MONDAY MARATHON, and a winners' rostrum, with 1, 2 and 3 painted on the steps.

I began to get a bit nervous, glancing towards the trees from where the runners were first going to appear. Had Jaz managed to hide herself all right? Suppose Bill had gone really *really* fast? What if there was some thing, some tiny thing, that we hadn't thought about?

I pushed myself into a crowd of people to hide.

"My Steven will win for sure," a woman was saying.

"I wouldn't be so certain," someone else said, "there are some very keen kids here. What about that young lad limbering up at the start doing press-ups? He looked fit."

"Some of the girls looked pretty good, too," I blurted out, and then quickly shrank away before they could see me properly.

I checked my watch: two-forty! At any minute now...

"I can see someone coming through the trees!" a man called.

"Is it our Steven?" said the woman.

I held my breath.

"No, it's not, it's one of the other boys!"

I spluttered and started to choke.

"Oh no, I'm wrong. It's a *girl*!"

And Jaz emerged from the trees, waving at the crowd!

Everyone cheered and clapped as she ran towards the flagpole. I cheered, but not so loudly as to make an exhibition of myself.

"Well, look at her – fresh as a daisy," someone said. "You'd never think she'd just run a marathon!"

Jaz got to the pole, then went off to give her name (my name) to the officials. A tall man spoke on a mobile phone to someone at the start to confirm what time she'd set off, and then I heard him say to Jaz, "Very well done indeed. You've broken our record by three minutes!"

Bill ran in about two minutes later to take second place. Jaz was standing behind someone when he arrived, and for a moment he didn't see her. When he did, though, he staggered back, and almost fell over.

"Whaa! I don't believe it!" he wailed. "How *could* you have..."

"Yes, I can't think how I made that time," I

heard her reply, "considering that I stopped twice to do up my shoelaces."

He gave a strangled cry which pleased me no end, and Jaz just smiled at him sweetly and went off for refreshments.

All there was for me to do then was keep in the background, wait for the prize-giving and hope that Jaz wouldn't say anything careless along the way. I squashed down a little sliver of guilt about winning a prize by cheating, and began to try and work out a way that the two of us could get out of the Park and into Dad's car without being seen.

By three forty-five all the runners, even the stragglers, were in and counted, and just before four o'clock the first, second and third prize-winners were called to take their places on the rostrum.

"In first place this week," announced a man in a white track suit, "in the remarkable time of forty-two minutes, is Miss Jenny May!"

Hearing my name, I almost jumped up to

get the prize, but remembered just in time that Jaz was still being me. Bill was called next, and then a boy named Nat.

As the white track suit man went up to Jaz (with Polly shouting, "Super! Well done that girl!"), I felt great. We'd done it! We'd managed to get through the weekend without being caught, we'd got the better of Bill *and* we'd won a prize. Best of all, in two hours' time Dad would be coming to take us home and the whole ordeal would be over.

The man shook Jaz's hand and said she could choose between four prizes, and then, *then*, up ran a tall woman with a smile on her face.

She took the microphone from the man. "I want to announce a special prize," she said. "Because our Monday Marathon winner today is *already* here as a prize-winner, we're going to give her something extra."

Ooh good, I thought, we'd have something each. We wouldn't have to fight over one pair of roller-blades.

"We'd like her – and the other three poetry prize-winners she's sharing her holiday with – to have another whole week in Paradise Park! Now, what d'you think of that?"

SPOOK SPOTTING
Mary Hooper

She spots them here, she spots them there, she spots those spooks most everywhere!

Going to stay in an old castle, ace spook-spotter Amy is hoping for headless ghosts, secret passages and blood-thirsty vampires. Her best friend Hannah, meanwhile, is on the lookout for rare birds.

As it turns out there are thrilling surprises in store for them both in this high-spirited and highly entertaining story.

SPOOKS AHOY!
Mary Hooper

When spook-spotting Amy takes to the river, her imagination goes overboard!

At the prospect of a boating holiday with Mum and best friend Hannah, Amy's mind is awash with dreams of treasure, mermaids, phantom ships and adventure on the high seas. The reality, however, is very different!

"A hilarious tale... Very funny and highly readable." *The Observer*

CREEPE HALL FOR EVER!
Alan Durant

Back once more at Creepe Hall, Oliver finds his relations in a gloomy mood. Uncle Vladimir is away and the odious Uncle Sylvester, Aunt Lupina and their horrible son Horace have taken up residence. To get rid of them, Oliver seeks a sporting solution – helped by Mummy, twins Con and Can, Werebadger, Cleopatra, Uncle Franklin and the latest Creepe-creation, Tiddles! But who will be victorious?

SEVEN WEIRD DAYS AT NUMBER 31
Judy Allen

The weird things start to happen as soon as Mike and his parents move into their new home, Number 31 South Street. Mike's clothes fly out of the window, footsteps pad up the stairs at night, the old clock sounds as though its chime has been turned off... The house is haunted, Mike is sure, and the ghost wants him out. But why and what can he do? Mike and his friend Scott have to solve the spooky mystery in this high-spirited ghost story by an award-winning author.